Notes from a pro

ABDO
Scan
to
Read

BAND GEEKS
NOTES FROM A PRO

Calico

An Imprint of Magic Wagon
www.abdopublishing.com

by Amy Cobb
Illustrated by Anna Cattish

www.abdopublishing.com

Published by Magic Wagon, a division of ABDO,
PO Box 398166, Minneapolis, Minnesota 55439.
Copyright © 2015 by Abdo Consulting Group, Inc.
International copyrights reserved in all countries. No part of this
book may be reproduced in any form without written permission from
the publisher. Calico™ is a trademark and logo of Magic Wagon.

Printed in the United States of America, North Mankato, Minnesota.
102014
012015

Written by Amy Cobb
Illustrations by Anna Cattish
Edited by Megan M. Gunderson & Bridget O'Brien
Cover and interior design by Candice Keimig

Library of Congress Cataloging-in-Publication Data

Cobb, Amy, author.
  Notes from a pro / by Amy Cobb ; illustrated by Anna Cattish.
    pages cm. -- (Band geeks)
  Summary: When one of the other members of Benton Bluff Junior
High band shows up with a shiny new trombone, Kori Neal's school-
loaner suddenly seems beat-up and old so she comes up with an idea
to organize a fund-raiser to buy new instruments--until advice from a
famous local jazz musician gives her a clearer perspective on the issue.
  ISBN 978-1-62402-075-9
  1. Bands (Music)--Juvenile fiction. 2. Musical instruments--Juvenile
fiction. 3. Jazz musicians--Juvenile fiction. 4. Money-making projects
for children--Juvenile fiction. 5. Junior high schools--Juvenile fiction. [1.
Bands (Music)--Fiction. 2. Musical instruments--Fiction. 3. Musicians-
-Fiction. 4. Fund raising--Fiction. 5. Junior high schools--Fiction. 6.
Schools--Fiction.] I. Cattish, Anna, illustrator. II. Title.
  PZ7.1.C63No 2015
  813.6--dc23
                                    2014033609

With extra special thanks to Larry Vaught for graciously
sharing his expertise and passion for music.
I am forever grateful to Clelia Gore, Megan Gunderson,
and Candice Keimig for taking a chance on me. —AC

TABLE OF CONTENTS

Chapter 1
SHOWING OFF

"Hey, I've got it!" Lemuel Soriano said, catching up with me by my locker. Lunch was over, and we were both headed to the band room.

"Whatever you've got, you can keep it, Lem." I covered my nose with my hand. "Because I don't want to get it."

"Kori!" He frowned. "I'm not sick."

"Just kidding." I moved my hand and pointed to my lips. "See? I'm smiling."

"Good." Lem's frown faded. "Because I'm talking about the challenge music Mr. Byrd asked us to work on. I practiced all night, and I skipped most of lunch to practice some more." Now Lem was the one smiling. "And I finally got it!"

"That's awesome!" I high-fived him. But I wasn't surprised. Lem practices harder than anybody else in the Benton Bluff Junior High band. He probably plays his trumpet more than he does anything. Even eating. Or sleeping.

"How about you? Did you practice?" Lem asked.

"Nope." I fidgeted with a loose thread on my backpack strap. Lem's lucky. I can't practice as much as he can.

"Kori!" Lem's brown eyes widened behind his blue-framed glasses.

"Hey, it's no biggie."

"Yeah," Lem said, "it is too. Mr. Byrd wants us to have this song ready for our final concert."

Okay, so Lem was right. It really was a big deal. Every year, Mr. Byrd, our band director, plans the Summer Celebration concert at our school for just before summer break. And he always puts together a special ensemble to play a harder arrangement that he calls a challenge song. This year, Mr. Byrd chose some kids from the brass section, including Lem. And me.

"I'll be ready," I promised. "I'll practice tonight." I wanted to, anyway, but I wasn't so sure it would happen.

"We're all counting on you," Lem said.

"I know."

But Lem wasn't the only one counting on me. Last night, my mom worked second shift at Dottie's Diner. So she'd counted on me to help my little brother and two little sisters with their homework. And then they counted on me to cook them supper. Hot dogs, macaroni and cheese, and toast have become my specialty, ever since my dad moved out.

Good thing no one's counting on *him*. Not anymore, anyway.

"You can count on me," I added. And I was serious. Helping out at home and preparing for the concert—somehow, I'd make it all work.

Lem held out his hand for a fist bump. "Don't let *moi* down."

"I won't." Our knuckles thumped together. "So is that the only French word you know, or what?"

"Of course not. After you, *mademoiselle*." Lem held the band room door open for me.

Lem is related to French royalty. But only by marriage. And that was so long ago cavemen still walked pet dinosaurs on leashes. Lem found out about his fancy ancestor when we studied our family trees. Now he throws in French words every chance he gets. Like now. All the way into the band room, Lem talked in an exaggerated French accent.

Lem is cool. At least, most of the time. Sometimes we don't get along so great. But that's because we both want to be the best in band. Being the best is easy for Lem. For me, not so much. Especially with Jack Cassilly III playing trombone, too. He's such a showboat. And today, he was at it again.

When Lem and I walked into the band room, half the band was gathered around Jack.

"What's Jack up to now?" Lem asked.

"Who knows?" But I was about to find out. "Excuse me, please," I said. "Comin' through."

"Watch it, Kori Neal!" Jack said. "You can't just plow your way through here with your raggedy old case."

"Hey, Jack Cassilly III, I'm just tryin' to get to my chair."

But when I got closer to my seat, I saw why everybody was gathered around Jack. In his hands was the shiniest, most perfectly gold trombone I'd ever seen. In my whole life.

Jack must've noticed me staring. "Impressive, isn't it? My parents special ordered it."

He held the mouthpiece up to his lips then, and a lock of blond hair fell across one of his blue eyes. He looked like he was posing for an ad in some band instrument catalog. That was Jack.

Mr. Perfect. Perfect hair. Perfect family. And now, perfect trombone.

"It's nice," I said. "Really nice."

"Yeah, too bad I'm stuck sitting next to you and your ratty school loaner." The tip of Jack's snobby nose was so far in the air it practically pointed at the ceiling lights.

I hugged my case against my chest. "There's nothing wrong with Russell." That's what I named

my trombone, after my dad. I pretty much only see my dad on holidays since he moved six hours away. I'm mad at him, but I miss him, too. So it makes me feel a little closer to him.

And anyway, Russell is like a friend. When Dad first left, playing my trombone helped me. A lot. I just wish I had more time to practice, like I used to before Mom got a full-time assistant manager job at Willard's Wash and Dry Laundromat and a part-time job at Dottie's Diner until she finds something that pays more.

"You're right," Jack finally agreed. "That'd be a great instrument if nobody'd landed on the moon yet. It's *so* ancient." Jack smiled, flashing his perfect white teeth. "We're talking a whole other century."

My eyes felt watery, but no matter how bad it got, I refused to cry in front of Jack. Instead, I opened my case and took out Russell.

I was glad when Mr. Byrd stepped onto the podium then and had us warm up with a concert

B-flat scale. I tried to do what I always do. I tried to ignore Jack.

It usually worked. But it was harder today. I couldn't ignore his new trombone. Even from the corner of my eye, it shined in the light. It was gorgeous. And I knew I'd never have an instrument like that.

About halfway through class, Mr. Byrd said, "Time out!" and made a T with his hands. "Do not look at your fingers, first-year students! They're not going anywhere." He took off his straw hat and fanned himself with it. "In fact, if this is your first year in band, let's chat," he said. "At my desk. On the double."

Kids scrambled up front.

"Everyone else, take five." Mr. Byrd slipped his hat back on his balding head.

Mr. Byrd looked like he was ready to kick back on the sand in his colorful beach umbrella shirt. Some kids joke that Mr. Byrd dresses like he's going on vacation, instead of taking a real one, because he's too tight to fork over the cash for a plane ticket.

But really, directing band is Mr. Byrd's life. Even in the summer, he helps run band camp. And he spends time tutoring kids who need extra help.

But the new kids this year had already found out that inside this band room, Mr. Byrd was a junior high band drill sergeant. Eventually, they'd find out that's only because he really loves music. And us. But he can still be super intimidating sometimes!

They were also figuring out that Mr. Byrd's "chats" were really lectures. And we all knew he'd take longer than five minutes. Jack got up to show off his new trombone to Jasper Fava in the percussion section. Then Lem grabbed Jack's seat.

"I heard what Jack said about your trombone earlier," Lem began. "Don't worry about him, Kori."

I tried to act cool about it. "*Pffft.* I'm not. No way."

Lem nodded. "Yeah, there's nothing wrong with Russell."

"Of course there isn't," I said, glancing down at Russell. "Except for some scratches here and there." And Russell is nowhere near as shiny as Jack's new trombone. And sometimes the mouthpiece gets stuck. And Russell's case really does look like it's been to the moon and back. And hit by an asteroid. Or two.

I rubbed my thumb back and forth across Russell's brace. "Lem, it's not fair. I've played a school loaner for two years. And I'd love to have a trombone like Jack's."

That isn't too much for an almost-eighth grader to wish for, right? I mean, c'mon! Next year would be my last in junior high band. But Lem looked at me like I was crazy.

"I know," I sighed. "It'll never happen. Jack's family is loaded, and mine is, well . . ."

Lem leaned back in Jack's chair.

We sat there for a couple of minutes, neither of us saying anything. I felt bad for even thinking about a new trombone, like I wasn't loyal to Russell. And I wished that I hadn't ever said anything out loud. I rubbed Russell's slide with the hem of my T-shirt, trying to make him just a little shinier.

"*Voilà!* I know!" Lem finally said. "Why don't you get a job, like walking dogs or something?"

"Good idea, but that wouldn't work. I'd have to take my brother and sisters with me," I said. "And they're sort of wild sometimes. I can just see 'em getting all tangled up in the leashes."

Then Lem flicked the loop his shoelace made. "Forget a job, Kori." He smacked his forehead. "I for real got it this time. A fund-raiser!"

"Nah, I don't know about that." I squirmed in my chair. "I couldn't stand people feeling all sorry for me and donating money."

"Not just for you," Lem said. "Some other kids could use new instruments, too."

That was true. Suddenly I realized how selfish I'd been. I needed to think bigger. I'm not the only one with a school loaner. Kelly Matson has a really old trumpet. And Alex Gamblin's French horn might've been hit by a couple of asteroids, too, just like Russell.

"So maybe we could raise some money for everyone," Lem went on.

"Have you ever looked at new instruments, Lem? They're not cheap."

"So we'll raise a *lot* of money!" he said.

"We'd have to if we we're gonna buy new instruments for everybody who needs one."

"I vote we talk to *Monsieur* Byrd about it. Are you in?" Lem held out his hand.

I thought about it for a minute. Then I put my hand on top of his. "Yeah." I smiled. "Count me in."

Then we raised our hands up in the air and finished with a funny handshake, wiggling our fingers to seal our deal.

Chapter 2
RAISING FUNDS

"Okay, everyone! We'll take it from the top." Mr. Byrd clapped then. His "chat" with the first-year band students had taken more like fifteen minutes than five.

Lem left and Jack sat beside me again.

"One and two and—" Mr. Byrd began.

ERRRR! The bell rang. Band was over.

"Remember to practice!" Mr. Byrd yelled as everyone quickly took apart their instruments. "And when you're finished, practice again!"

Jack stood up, holding his new trombone like a trophy. Then he looked down at me. "All the practice in the world won't help you on your old trombone." Then he laughed.

Ignore. Ignore. Ignore.

If I wasn't totally sure before, I was now. Lem's fund-raising idea was perfect. Hopefully Mr. Byrd would back us up.

When the band room cleared out, Lem said, "Mr. Byrd, can we talk to you?"

"Certainly." He pushed up his glasses and looked from Lem to me. "Is everything okay?"

"Yes, sir," Lem said.

Mr. Byrd knows Lem and I are competitive. But this time, we were both on the same side. And I smiled to prove we weren't arguing.

"Wonderful!" Mr. Byrd looked relieved. "So is this about playing your challenge music?"

"No, sir," Lem said. "I've already got mine."

Mr. Byrd looked at me.

"And I'll get mine." I'd make time to practice. Somehow.

"Then how may I help you?" Mr. Byrd asked.

"It's sort of how we can help the band," Lem began.

Mr. Byrd's eyebrows shot up. "Really?"

"Yeah, some of our school-loaner instruments are really old," I added.

"So we thought we'd hold some fund-raisers," Lem said.

I tucked my hair behind my ear. "To make some cash to buy new ones."

Mr. Byrd held up his hands. "Hang on, guys. New instruments are really expensive."

"That's what I told him." I pointed at Lem.

"So we'll just have to raise a lot of money," Lem said.

I nodded. "A whole lot."

"I'm not sure if raising that much money is possible," Mr. Byrd said. "There are several school loaners in the band."

I patted Russell's case. "I know."

"But can we try, *monsieur*?" Lem asked.

A picture of Jack with his new trombone popped into my brain. "Please," I said, crossing my fingers.

Mr. Byrd looked unsure at first. "Fund-raisers are hard work," he began. "I'm not sure if you know what you're getting into."

Now I was pretty sure fund-raising was a no go.

"But I admire that you two are willing to work together. And that you want to help your peers."

Or was it?

"Does that mean we can do it?" I asked.

"Hang on! I don't want you to be disappointed if you're not able to get new instruments for everyone." Mr. Byrd continued. "But with that in mind, why not give it a go? See what happens!"

"Yes!" Lem high-fived me.

"And," Mr. Byrd added, "you two are in charge of all the planning."

"*Oui! Merci!*" Lem said. "That means yes and thank you!"

I added, "Thanks, Mr. Byrd!"

Then Mr. Byrd gave Lem and me hall passes. But I could hardly concentrate on adverbs in Mrs.

Tudor's English class. All I could think about was band.

Look out, Jack Cassilly III! His new trombone was going to have company. I couldn't wait to get started planning the fund-raisers.

The next day, while Mr. Byrd ran through some exercises with the newer band students, Lem and I talked about fund-raising with some of the others.

"So are we raising funds to have a party?" Zac Wiles asked. "I vote for a pizza party! Who doesn't love pizza?"

Zac is always goofing off. All he thinks about is having fun. And parties.

"No, Zac," I said. "We want to raise money to buy some new instruments to replace the old school loaners," I said.

"No party?" Zac asked.

I shook my head. "Sorry."

"Man!" Zac snapped his fingers. "But I hope we have a bake sale, at least. I can be in charge of taste testing all the cookies."

I smiled. "I'll remember that, Zac."

Baylor Meece asked, "Seriously, what kind of fund-raisers would we do?"

"That's what we wanted to talk about," Lem said. "We want to hear everybody's ideas."

"Right," I chimed in.

"Maybe we could sell candy bars," Hope James suggested.

"Hey, candy works for me, too!" Zac grinned.

"But everybody does that," Baylor said.

"True. We need something special," Hope said.

"How about a dance-a-thon?" Sherman Frye said. "I could show off my moves. Check out the sprinkler, Sherman-style." He stood up, grabbed one ankle, and sort of hopped around while pointing at us. Sherman is big time into fitness, even yoga and dancing.

"Um, maybe not that different, Sherman," Baylor said, changing her mind.

"A car wash?" Zac asked.

Baylor frowned. "Everybody does those, too."

"I have an idea," I said.

Everyone looked at me.

I tucked my hair behind my ear. "What if we did some kind of doggie dog wash? We could bathe and groom dogs," I said.

"Sort of like a salon for dogs?" Sherman said.

"Yep, exactly." I nodded.

"I like it!" Lem smiled. "But why stop at just dogs? Why not groom cats? Or rabbits, even?"

"Rabbits need love, too!" Zac joked.

"We could call it Pampered Pets," I suggested.

"That's perfect, Kori!" Hope said. "You have tons of good ideas. How come I never knew that?"

"I dunno." I smiled and shrugged my shoulders.

"Yeah, Quiet Kori doesn't usually say much," Baylor said.

"Maybe she can't talk because you two are always talking." Zac opened and closed his hands like they were talking mouths.

Baylor poked Zac's ribs.

"Hey, I'm kidding!" Zac said.

They were right, though, about me not talking a lot. I mean, I used to when I was younger. And then Dad left. At first, I thought it was my fault. Like he left because I did something wrong.

After a while, I figured out it wasn't my fault. But by then everybody had labeled me Quiet Kori. It just got easier not to say much. I figured if I didn't have a lot of friends, I wouldn't get hurt. Easy.

"You're gonna have to start talking more, Kori," Baylor said.

"Yeah," Hope agreed.

I shrugged again. But I wondered if they were right. Maybe I would talk more. Maybe.

"Well, right now we need to talk about a second fund-raiser," Lem said. "How about a garage sale?"

"You mean sell our old junk?" Sherman asked.

"Hey, my stuff's not junk," Zac said.

"One guy's trash is another guy's treasure," Baylor said.

Then everybody started talking all at once about what they had to sell. Everybody except Jack. He hadn't said a word this whole time.

"Excuse me!" Mr. Byrd said. "We're working on timing over here. If we could hear ourselves, that is." Then he turned an imaginary volume button. "Dial it down."

"Sorry, *monsieur*," Lem said.

Mr. Byrd turned back around.

Lem said, more quietly now, "So is everybody in for Pampered Pets and a garage sale?"

"Sure," Sherman said.

Hope nodded. "Me too!"

"I'm there," Baylor said. "And I can even write an article about the fund-raisers for the *Bloodhound*." That's our school paper. Baylor is our best reporter.

"Count me in as long as somebody still brings cookies," Zac said.

"Zac!" Baylor shook her head.

Lem looked at me. "What about you, Kori?"

"Definitely," I said. We'd have to plan them on days Mom wasn't working. But I didn't say that.

That just left Jack.

"Are you in, Jack?" Lem asked.

"Whatever." Jack crossed his arms. "I'll be there if I don't have something better to do."

Jack Cassilly III wouldn't show up. I knew it.

Chapter 3
PAMPERED PETS

The next weekend, it was Mom's day off. And we were running late. But we finally pulled into the parking lot at a local vet clinic for the band's Pampered Pets fund-raiser.

"Ready, Kori?" Mom asked.

"Yep, I think so."

"Okay, I'll see you this afternoon! Have fun. And good luck!" Mom waved as she drove off.

Most of the band was already there, gathered around a table piled high with pet grooming supplies. A water hose stretched across the sidewalk to a couple of huge silver tubs filled with water, warming in the sun.

"Sorry I'm late," I said, joining them.

"What took you so long?" Lem asked.

"I couldn't leave until Mom scrambled eggs for someone who doesn't even exist."

"Huh?" Hope asked.

"My brother, Evan, ate all of the Yummy-O Bitz for breakfast. And then my baby sister, Leah, went crazy because there was no cereal left for Chloe, her imaginary friend," I explained. "Luckily, there were two eggs still left in the fridge. And double lucky, I don't mind scrambled eggs."

Hope nodded. "I had an imaginary friend once."

"I still do!" Zac said.

"Zac!" Baylor nudged him.

"What? You don't believe me?" He grinned.

Baylor shook her head.

"Hey, look!" Lem pointed to a dusty car pulling up beside us. "We have our first customer!"

"Already?" I glanced at my watch. It was only nine o'clock. This day was starting off right! Maybe a new trombone would be easier to get than I'd hoped.

The car window zipped down. All that could be seen above the door was a pair of old-lady glasses and little bitty rollers all over her gray head. I wasn't sure how she could see over the steering wheel.

"Car wash?" she asked.

"Doggie wash," Lem said. "We're raising money for our school band."

"I don't have a dog, dear," she said.

"It doesn't have to be a dog! Our fund-raiser is called Pampered Pets, and we'll pamper your pet. Any pet," I said. I wanted our fund-raiser to be a success. So I couldn't be Quiet Kori today. And we couldn't just let our first customer get away.

But she wasn't interested. Her rollers bobbed up and down as she drove over a speed bump and back onto the main road.

Zac snapped his fingers. "Told ya we should've had a car wash."

"It's okay," Baylor said.

"*Oui*," Lem agreed. "It's still early."

"People are probably sleeping in since it's Saturday," I said.

"If it wasn't for this dumb fund-raiser, I'd be sleeping, too."

Jack? He came strolling toward us. I was surprised he even showed up. I really hadn't thought he would.

"I don't see why I should have to help out anyway," Jack went on.

"It's called helping out your fellow band mates, Jack," Hope said.

He shrugged. "Whatever. It's not like *I* need a new instrument."

No, he really didn't. And the way Jack was acting, I wished he'd stayed home with his new trombone instead of bothering to show up here.

Pretty soon, Mr. Byrd stopped by, too, holding a couple of shopping bags. "How's it going?"

"Not good," I said. "So far, we haven't had a single customer."

"I'm sorry. Keep in mind, fund-raisers require patience." Then Mr. Byrd held up the shopping bags. "Maybe these will boost your spirits."

Lem peeked inside. "Donuts!"

"Yum! Dibs on a chocolate one," I said. "Thank you, sir."

Everyone else thanked him, too, and we all dug in until nothing was left but crumbs.

"Now I'm thirsty," Lem said.

"Me too. Good thing we have water." Zac reached for the hose and we all took turns drinking from it, except Jack. He drank the organic apple juice he'd brought with him.

Then Zac decided making "rain" would be fun. He pointed the hose up toward the sky and turned it on and off, on and off, letting the drops fall on the shrubs growing along the sidewalk. But then it "rained" on our heads.

"Okay, that's enough, Zac. You're wasting water," Mr. Byrd said.

"But we haven't washed any animals yet." Zac folded his arms across his camouflage shirt. "So are we really wasting water? Or are we saving it?"

"Off! Now!" Mr. Byrd said.

"Yes, sir." Zac didn't waste time doing it.

Closer to lunch, things picked up a little. We washed a boxer puppy who had gotten a little too nervous during his vet exam.

Then Lem's dad brought over Gabby, their Shar-Pei mix. He had felt sorry for us when he drove by and saw we didn't exactly have a line of customers. We had to wash every single one of Gabby's wrinkles. And dry them, too. *Ew.* Believe me, we earned our twelve bucks.

After lunch, we groomed our first pet that wasn't a dog.

"How much to wash my guinea pig?" a little boy asked.

"We're working for donations," I said. "So whatever you want to give us."

"Okay," the kid said.

So Lem put a little bit of warm water in the bottom of a small tub. I grabbed the shampoo.

"What's your guinea pig's name?" Lem asked.

"Gill," the kid said.

"That's cute," I said.

But Gill didn't act cute. Every time I went to rub shampoo into his fur, he charged the washcloth and hissed. Then he hopped around like popping popcorn kernels. Trust me, slippery guinea pigs are hard to hang on to.

Baylor and Hope came over to help out. It took three of us to give one little guinea pig a bath. And afterward, we only got $1.39.

"That's all I have," the kid said, grabbing Gill when he was clean, dried, and fluffy. "But thanks! Gill looks beautiful."

Jack walked over then. "So when's this thing going to be over? I have better things to do than watch you wrestle guinea pigs."

"You could help us, you know," Lem said.

Tell him, Lem. All day, Jack had sat around doing nothing. Except complaining. He just watched the rest of us work when we actually had customers.

We were just about to call it a day when we got one more customer. I almost didn't recognize her without her rollers. It was the little old lady who was looking for a car wash this morning. She still didn't have a dog, but she was back with her cat.

"Boopsie just loves water." She nuzzled the cat.

Boopsie meowed. But when her kitty paw pads hit the soap suds, she morphed into Evil Boopsie. And my arms became Boopsie's personal scratching posts.

"Hey, everybody, how is Kori like her trombone? They're both covered in horrible marks!" Jack laughed.

"Ha-ha," I said. "Very funny." But it wasn't. At all. Jack's lame joke cut me deeper than any cat claws ever could. Not that I would ever let him see that.

So we finished the day with $28.17. We would've had a little more, but Mr. Byrd went across the street to buy a box of band-aids for me. Thanks a lot, Boopsie. Our band garage sale had to turn out better than this.

Chapter 4

EVERYTHING MUST GO!

The band planned our garage sale for the next weekend at Baylor's house since she lived in a big subdivision. The morning started off rainy. Real rain this time, not rain from a hose courtesy of Zac. But then the sun popped out, and so did garage salers. So we finished setting up our stuff.

Hope hung a yellow sweater on a hanger. "I can't believe I ever wore this."

"Me either," Zac said. "It's so bright I almost need Kori's sunglasses to look at it."

"Two dollars," I held them up, "and they're yours."

"Will you take Monopoly cash?" Zac reached for the stack of games Lem had for sale.

I smiled. "Not today."

"I'd talk, Zac," Baylor cut in. "Everything you're selling is camouflage. Boots and caps. Even your shirts. And look!" She peeked at Zac through a giant hole cut up the side. "Why do you cut up your shirts?"

Zac snatched it back. "Hey, that's cool. And they keep me cool when I'm working out." He flexed his muscles.

"I didn't know you work out," Lem said.

"He just started yesterday, Lem. Can't you tell?" Baylor joked.

"Can't you tell?" Zac mimicked Baylor. "And what are you laughing at me for? Check out this purse with the flying pigs with rainbow wings all over it." He pranced across the garage with it slung over his shoulder.

Then Zac clipped on a pair of shiny silver and purple dress-up earrings that Hope was selling. He grabbed one of Hope's old dolls, too, and patted her back, pretending to burp her. Except Zac really did burp. "Excuse you," he said to the doll, and then he laughed at his own joke.

"Gimme it!" Baylor laughed, trying to get her purse.

Hope was reaching for her stuff and laughing at Zac, too.

"Kids, behave!" Baylor's mom, Marcie, stood in the garage then. But she was smiling at Zac's fashion show, too. "You have customers!" She pointed.

Yulia Glatt and Davis Beadle got some interest in the comics they had displayed on a table. And someone was checking out Sherman's old yo-yos.

"Can you kids help me for a sec?" Marcie asked. "I've been going through some stuff, and I have a lot of junk to donate to your cause."

"Shhh," I said, looking around. "Don't let the customers hear you call this stuff junk. I saw it on TV. You really gotta talk stuff up so people buy it."

"Oh, right," Marcie said. "Then can you help me
carry this super, fantastic, amazing stuff out to the
garage?"

"Yes, ma'am." Zac jumped up to help. So did
Baylor, Hope, and Lem. I followed, too.

"Wow! You weren't joking," I said when we
walked into the den. "You do have a lot of stuff."
Plates, cups, pots and pans, lamps, flower pots,
and even a chair were heaped into a pile.

"It looks like you're selling half your kitchen," Hope said.

"She may as well," Baylor said. "It's not like she ever cooks when she's in there."

Baylor's mom squeezed her shoulders. "You're right. That's what we have your dad for." And she winked.

"Hey, I could go for some of your dad's cupcakes," Zac said.

"Me too!" I agreed.

Baylor's dad runs a bakery. So her dad always brings yummy cupcakes to our school parties.

"C'mon," Marcie said. "There's no time for cupcake talk when you've got all of this awesome merchandise to sell."

"That's right," I said.

"Yeah, I hope we make a lot of money this week," Kelly Matson said. She and Alex Gamblin came over to help then.

"Me too." Alex nodded. "I could use a new French horn. I think mine was the first one ever invented."

I smiled. I really, really hoped we'd earn enough for all of us to get new instruments. I mean, I knew it wouldn't happen today. But maybe we'd at least get off to a good start.

So Lem and Zac moved the chair, while the rest of us grabbed some boxes and headed back out to the garage.

I organized seasonal decorations into holiday displays on a table. We had Thanksgiving, Christmas, and Valentine's Day sections. "Everything must go!" I announced to browsing customers.

Quiet Kori wasn't at Pampered Pets, and I'd made up my mind that she wouldn't show up at this sale either. This was for the band. "Check out these bargains!" I went on.

"Looking good, Kori!" Baylor's mom said, walking past.

"Thanks!" I said. It did look sort of professional. Well, as professional as it could with crazy hats on one side and a fish tank on the other.

Lem had whipped out a calculator. Since he was the smartest person in band, he was in charge of collecting the money we made.

"How are we doing so far?" I asked.

"So far," Lem pushed a couple more buttons on the calculator, "we have $43.65, *mademoiselle*."

"Hey, that's better than last weekend," I said.

"Yeah, and you don't even have to fight a cat for it."

I looked down at the fading scratches Boopsie had left on my arms. "Yeah, or listen to Jack either."

Lem nodded. "But it's still early. Jack might show up."

I hoped not. I'd rather give Boopsie a bath every single day than listen to Jack complaining about our fund-raisers for even five more minutes. But this day was about earning money for new instruments, not worrying about Jack.

For the next few hours, I turned into a real saleswoman, a sort of walking, talking billboard. I took an item we had for sale and carried it around to show it off to the customers. And when it sold, I grabbed something else.

It really worked, too. My roller blades skated off with a teenager. Sherman's yoga DVDs were just what a yoga-loving granny had been looking for. Even Lem's old remote control cars with their bent antennas, Zac's cracked tackle box, Davis's hamster wheel, and Baylor's lava lamp—SOLD!

By that afternoon, we'd made a grand total of $153.75. Sure, it wasn't enough to buy even one new instrument, but it wasn't a bad start either. And maybe the best part was that hanging out with the band kids had been fun. For the first time since Dad left, I felt like I sort of had friends.

"Hey, nice of you to show up when we're cleaning up," Zac said.

I whirled around to see who he was talking to.

Jack.

"I didn't want to waste my day on another dumb fund-raiser that bombed," Jack said.

"We did well today," Hope said. "And you should've seen Kori work the crowd."

"She was pretty awesome," Baylor added.

"You want to know what's awesome?" Jack smirked. "Private music lessons. That's where *I've* been today."

A new trombone. And private lessons, too?

"Nobody's going to be better in the trombone section than me." Jack looked at me then. "Nobody. And since this is a junk sale, I hope you sold your trombone today."

"Russell's not junk," I said. But really, when I said it, I wasn't so sure I believed it myself. I eyed the box that held the cash we'd made today. I mean, if Russell wasn't junk, then why was I trying to earn money for a new instrument?

Chapter 5
JAZZ FRONT

Even though the band didn't raise enough money to buy even one new instrument, a few days later I decided to go check them out anyway. Maybe when I saw the price tag on a new trombone, I'd convince my brain to forget all about getting one. And I'd be happy playing Russell again, just like I was before Jack showed up with his new trombone.

So after school, I biked over to a new music store a couple of blocks from our apartment. Ivy climbed up the red brick toward the JAZZ FRONT shop sign. A drum set was on display in the window, along with a Blowout Sale advertisement. In one corner was a Help Wanted sign.

The bell above the door jingled as I walked in.

"Howdy do!" the man behind the counter said, straightening his bow tie.

"Hey!" I stopped in my tracks. "I remember you. You're Mr. Chenault. You helped judge solo auditions at my school a couple of months ago."

He was a famous local jazz musician, too. But I didn't know this was his shop.

"You may call me Rube." He smiled. "Now, refresh my memory. Which school was it?"

"Benton Bluff Junior High," I said.

"Um, hmm," he said. "Your band director is Mr. Byrd. A fine young man and a fine bunch of kids, as I recollect."

That was mostly true, except the part about Mr. Byrd being young. I mean, his old band jacket says Class of '92. But I guess to someone as old as Rube, even fifty might still be young.

"And who might you be?" Rube asked.

"I'm Kori."

"And do you have a last name, Kori?" He smiled again.

"Neal, sir."

"Well, don't just stand there, Miss Kori Neal. Come on in here and tell me how I can help you today," Rube said.

I moved away from the door then and propped my elbows on the counter in front of Rube. Inside the glass were some vintage jazz photos and albums. Even the cash register looked old.

"Wait! Don't tell me," Rube said. "You came in here to look at trombones, didn't you?"

"Whoa. How'd you know?"

"In here hums a computer." Rube pointed to his silvery head. "I remember you now from the auditions. You really made that trombone of yours sing."

"I did?"

Another customer came over then to buy a pair of drumsticks.

"Excuse me, Kori."

While Rube rang up the sale, I checked out the shop. Guitars, saxophones, and just about any other instrument you could think of hung on the walls. Shelves were lined with extra reeds and instrument care items, like swabs and oil for valves.

There were gifts like T-shirts and mugs with music notes printed on them. There was a whole section of music to buy. And there was a section of old records and some new CDs, including Rube's.

But what I stared at the most was a shiny new trombone displayed on the wall. Wow! It was perfect. Just like Jack's. I could even see my reflection in it, like looking into a funny mirror. And I could see the price tag dangling from the slide: $1,000.

I stared at that trombone so long that Rube was busy with a new customer. So I sat at a table beneath a window and browsed through a jazz band book.

After a few minutes, Rube came over and sat across from me. "You like that song, do you?"

I glanced up from the measure I'd been looking at. "Oh, I don't know this song."

"I'm talking about *that* song." He pointed to the speaker above our heads. "You're certainly tapping your toes along."

I looked down at my feet. "I am?" I laughed. "I didn't even notice."

"That's jazz for you. It reaches straight into your heart and soul. And even your toes." He smiled. "So we were talking about trombones, weren't we?"

I nodded.

"I was impressed with your musical abilities at that solo audition."

"Seriously?" I impressed Rube Chenault?

"Hoo-wee! Yes, siree!" Rube smacked his knee.

"And that was with me playing Russell. What if I played one of those shiny new instruments on display?" I pointed to a trombone.

"Whoa, whoa, whoa. Back it up just a minute here." Rube's forehead creased. "Now, who's this Russell?"

I smiled. "Russell is my trombone."

"I see." Rube nodded.

"But Russell's a really old school loaner." Then I told him all about Jack's new trombone and how the band held some fund-raisers to try to buy new instruments. But we didn't make enough. And even if we had a fund-raiser every week, it would take us from now until we graduated from high school to replace the school loaners for everyone. I even told him how Jack called Russell junk.

Rube didn't say anything.

"So if I had a new trombone, I could play even better," I added.

"Kori," Rube began, "it's not just the instrument. It's the musician behind the instrument. And the heart beating inside the musician. Do you understand what I'm saying to you?"

Now it was my turn not to say anything.

"There's nothing wrong with your trombone, besides being old." The corners of Rube's eyes crinkled then when he smiled. "And some things get better with age," he said, winking.

I wanted to listen to Rube. Really. But Rube didn't have to sit in the trombone section with Jack Cassilly III. And I did.

I didn't stay long after that. Mom worked first shift at the diner today. That meant she'd be home for supper with my brother, sisters, and me. And that didn't happen too often.

But the closer I got to our apartment building, the more upset I got. By the time I closed our apartment door behind me, I really needed to talk to Mom. I was glad she was home.

"You look like you need a hug, sweetie." Mom wrapped her arms around me.

Definitely! I rested my head on her shoulder. She smelled like greasy burgers and fries, the way she always does after her diner shift. But it was familiar. And it was Mom. I liked it. I nestled even closer.

"Rough day?" she asked.

I nodded.

Mom held my hand and led me over to our faded couch. She plopped down and patted the cushion beside her. "Wanna talk about it?"

I told Mom all about Jack and how our fundraisers had flopped, the same story I'd told Rube earlier.

It would've been easier if I'd recorded the whole thing and just played it back. Except now the story had a different ending. I added in the part about stopping by Rube's shop.

"So basically, I stopped in there for nothing," I said. "And who knows? Maybe Rube is just some crazy old man who doesn't even have a clue what he's talking about."

Mom shook her head. "I don't think so. Crazy old men aren't usually successful jazz musicians who own their own music shops, are they?"

"No, I guess not." *Ugh. How come moms are always right about stuff like this?*

"So are you planning another fund-raiser?" Mom asked. "Maybe a bake sale? I could bake my famous chocolate chip brownies to help out."

"Nah, but thanks anyway. We'd have to bake enough brownies to sell for the next, like, ninety-three years to raise all the money we need."

Mom patted my shoulder. "How about if I bake some especially for you then?"

"And me!" My sister Elsie peeked around the corner.

"What have I told you about eavesdropping, young lady?" Mom hid a smile. "And have you picked up the toys on your side of the room?"

Elsie nodded and hopped up on the couch.

"So," Mom continued, kicking off her shoes

and propping her feet up on the coffee table, "are fund-raisers out?"

"Mom, your feet!" I said, ignoring her question. "What happened?"

She turned her ankles sideways, inspecting them. "They're just a little swollen from standing on them all day. It's no big deal."

"It looks like a big deal to me." A big, fat, swollen deal. "I wish you didn't have to work two jobs."

Mom shrugged. "It's only until something better comes along." She pushed my hair behind my ear. "And we were talking about you. So what's your next fund-raising plan?"

"I don't know. I thought seeing a new trombone at the music shop would help. Like my brain would see the price tag and say, 'Forget it!' But now, it's not just my brain that wants it. My heart does, too." I sighed. "And I know it'll never happen."

Mom looked down. Then with one red fingernail, she traced the outline of a rose that bloomed on the fabric of a pillow. The flower matched the couch color.

My mind flashed back to the day Mom bought it from a thrift shop. She'd been so excited to get a good deal. We even had money left over to splurge on ice cream cones on the way home.

That was a long time ago. It's been a while since we've had cones from an ice cream parlor.

But we've been in a lot of thrift shops since then. That's where we do all of our shopping. When it comes to antiques and vintage stuff, no joke, Mom seriously knows a lot. And I like learning about them, too.

Sometimes Mom and I even pretend we're cohosts of our own TV show and we're hunting for our next big find to share with fans. It makes shopping for used stuff more fun, especially when we get funny looks from other shoppers.

One time, this guy in a thrift shop asked us to interview him, like he thought there was really a camera hiding somewhere beneath the huge pile of used socks beside us. Mom and I had to leave because we couldn't stop laughing.

"I'm sorry, honey," Mom finally said. "Maybe you can put a new trombone on your someday wish list." She tried to smile. But she dabbed one eye with the back of her hand, like she was wiping away a tear.

Now I felt bad for even wanting something as expensive as a new trombone. Mom worked hard, and she did the best she could. I knew that.

"It's okay, Mom. Really." And I meant it. Because I had just made up my mind about something.

And that something was that Jack Cassilly III and his new trombone weren't going to bother me. Not anymore. Starting the next day in band.

Chapter 6
BAND JERK JACK

Mr. Byrd stood on the podium in the center of the room. Our chairs were arranged in a half-circle around him. We'd already warmed up and moved on to rehearsing some songs in our folders for the upcoming concert.

"I'm not picking on anyone," Mr. Byrd said, "but stop speeding up. This is the beat." He snapped his fingers then, accenting each word. "Don't. Go. Faster. Than. This."

Preparing for concerts can make Mr. Byrd crabby, but only because he wants us to do our best. So the crabs on his shirt today were a perfect fit. "From the top!" And he counted for us to begin.

"Better! Much better!" Mr. Byrd said. "Now flip to page three. We're going to take this song section by section, starting with the clarinets." He turned his attention to the front row.

Since Mr. Byrd wasn't working us right then, Jack made a big show of taking a cloth from his case and shining his trombone. "I don't like smudges on my *new* instrument," he said.

Then he held the cloth out to me. "Need to borrow this?" When I looked at him, he snatched it back. "Sorry, never mind. Cleaning your trombone won't help it look any better. Nothing will." And he shoved the cloth back into his case.

My face heated up. It was probably as red as the crabs on Mr. Byrd's shirt. But I refused to let Jack get to me. Nope. Not happening.

"Flutes!" Mr. Byrd called out.

Jack wasn't done trying to bug me, though. "Too bad about the fund-raisers." He stuck his bottom lip up over his top one, faking a sad face. "Guess you're stuck with that ratty old trombone, huh?"

I stared dead ahead, listening to the saxophone players now.

"I guess you could try to take private lessons, like me." Jack shook his head. "But my teacher would probably laugh if you walked through the door with that old piece of scrap metal."

That one stung. *Ignore, ignore, ignore.*

"Trumpets, you're up!" Mr. Byrd said.

As the trumpet players blew into their mouthpieces, I wondered something then. Was Jack this mean to everybody? Or was I just that special? But really, now that I thought about it, the only time that Jack acted like a jerk was in band. Then he became Band Jerk Jack.

Then Mr. Byrd said, "Trombones, let's hear it!"

At least Jack couldn't bug me while we played. I wished the measures on this page went on and on, all the way to the end of class. But the song ended. I figured Mr. Byrd would move on to the French horns then, but he didn't.

Instead, he said, "Kori, would you play that part one more time? By yourself, please."

Jack sort of snickered.

Great. I must've really hacked up the song. But I buzzed my lips into the mouthpiece and began to play it again. This time, I really, really didn't want the song to end. I was afraid of what Mr. Byrd would say when I stopped playing.

"Did you hear that?" Mr. Byrd said. "Kori played the loud notes LOUD!" He boomed. "And the soft notes *soft*," he whispered.

Then Mr. Byrd hopped off the podium and faced the whiteboard. He scrawled big blue capital letters across it. "Folks, we call that dynamics." He even underlined it before saying, "Kori is the Dynamics Master, and it's something I want you all to work on." Mr. Byrd stepped back onto the podium then and moved on. "Hit it, French horns!"

Lem gave me a thumbs-up. And Hope and Baylor both turned around in their chairs and smiled at me. I couldn't keep from smiling, too. Coming from Mr. Byrd, that was a huge compliment.

When I glanced at Jack, though, he wasn't smiling. And I got a bad feeling then. Things with Jack might be about to get even worse, if that was possible.

After each section had played through the measures, everyone played the song together a few more times as a group.

"Ah, hear that?" Mr. Byrd cupped a hand behind one ear. "That's music to my ears. Much better! That sounds like musicians ready to show off a year's worth of hard work at the Summer Celebration! And," he looked at his watch, "that's a wrap. Clean your instruments and head out, people."

I emptied Russell's spit valve and put him back in my case. I was about to close the latch when Jack started in. Again.

"Hey, Kori. My teacher said the same thing about me at my private lesson yesterday that Mr. Byrd just said about you. She said she'd never had a student play dynamics like I do." Jack even demonstrated, piano to forte.

"Nice," I said. I mean, what else was I supposed to say to that?

It was almost like Jack wanted to be in some sort of weird competition with me. But I couldn't figure out why he cared so much. It was crazy, but I just kept talking to him. "You know, Jack, you're the one with the new trombone *and* the private music lessons." *Hello! I don't have either!* "So I don't get why you seem so worried about me all the time."

"Me? Worried about you?" Jack fake laughed. As in bent over, clutching his stomach laughed. "Now that's funny!"

I didn't see anything funny about it. At all.

"I laughed until I cried." Jack made a show of wiping tears from his eyes. Then he shook his head like he felt sorry for me. "It's really too bad about your mom."

"What are you talking about, Jack?"

"You know." He shrugged. "If she worked harder, you could have a new trombone and private lessons, too."

That was too far. "You don't have a clue what you're even talking about! My mom works two jobs *and* takes care of me and my siblings." I wanted to twist his new trombone into a giant gold pretzel. "Money might buy new instruments and private lessons. But you know what it can't buy?"

Jack's nose pointed even higher in the air. "What?"

"Talent! And," I pointed to Jack's nose, "you might want to grab a tissue. Money's not the only thing that's green, you know."

"What are you, like, still in kindergarten?" Jack rolled his eyes. "Seriously, Kori. Don't let what Mr. Byrd said go to your head."

He might've acted like he didn't believe that last part I told him about the tissue. But when I left the

band room, I looked back. And guess what I saw?
Jack Cassilly III mining for green gold. Seriously.

After school, I walked home with Lem. And
with Russell. Trust me, lugging around a trombone
isn't easy. No wonder so many kids go for flutes
and clarinets in their cute little cases.

When we turned onto Lem's block, he said,
"Don't forget to practice your challenge music
tonight. Our concert is only a few weeks away."

"I won't forget. You remind me all the time. Like,
every single day."

"That's because I want us to be the *crème de la crème*." Lem smiled. "The best."

"I want us to be the whipped cream, too," I joked.

Lem laughed. "*Au revoir*, Kori." He waved goodbye.

"See ya tomorrow."

I was almost home when I thought about what Jack had said. The part about Mr. Byrd calling me the Dynamics Master and not letting it go to my head. Besides Mom and Mr. Byrd, Rube was the only other person who really ever told me I was good at playing the trombone. I needed Rube's help, so I texted Mom to let her know I'd be a little late getting home.

Chapter 7
ONE SPIFFY T-BONE

The bells above my head jingled when I opened the door of Jazz Front. But I didn't see Rube anywhere. So I set Russell down at my feet and pushed the bell on the counter beside a note that read Ring for Service.

"Kori!" Rube said when he saw me. "What a surprise! And what brings you in today?"

"This." I heaved Russell's case onto the counter and unlatched it. "Rube, meet Russell."

Rube looked at Russell, but he didn't say a word.

"The other day when I was in here, you said there was nothing wrong with Russell," I reminded him, gesturing toward my trombone.

I bet Rube didn't think that now. He only said there was nothing wrong with Russell because when he judged the solo competition at school, he didn't get a close-up look at him. Now he did. And I bet it would prove that Jack was right. Russell really was junk.

"And I still say there's nothing wrong with this trombone. But you thought I was a crazy old coot when you left here, didn't you?" He raised his eyebrows in question, but I couldn't answer.

I hung my head and stared at my sneakers. I had told Mom he was crazy when I got home that day. And if I looked at Rube, he'd know the truth.

Rube laughed. "It's okay. Wouldn't be the first time I've been called crazy." He pulled a pencil from behind his ear and set it on the counter. "Let me get out from behind here and I'll take a closer look at Mr. Russell."

Rube looked over his shoulder, toward what looked like a break room. "June, wait on the customers for me, would you, please? I think I'm going to be a little while."

When Rube opened the door that swung out from behind the counter, a black dog with graying paws and ears followed on his heels.

"You have a dog?" I said.

Rube glanced behind him. "Yes, siree, that's Mel." He reached down to scratch the dog's ears. "She's a good girl."

"A girl named Mel?"

Rube grinned. "It's short for Melody." Then he picked up Russell's case and I followed him over to the table beneath the window, where we'd sat the last time I stopped in. The Blowout Sale sign was gone, but the Help Wanted sign hadn't gone anywhere.

While Rube checked out Russell, I gave Mel a belly rub.

"Watch it now," Rube said. "You're gonna put her to sleep. And when she sleeps, she snores louder than any tuba I ever heard."

I laughed. "How come I didn't see her last time?"

"These days, Mel takes it easy. She mostly lounges around in the break room. Her big fluffy pillow's fit for a queen, I tell you." Rube stretched his arms out wide to show how big Mel's pillow was. "See that gray on her muzzle, Kori?"

I nodded.

"Mel's getting on in years. But inside that chest beats the most loyal heart I've ever known." Rube's eyes crinkled up at the corners when he talked about her. "Now," he said, "back to another old guy, Russell here."

I was starting to think Rube had a soft spot for old stuff. He held up Russell, slowly turning and studying each part in the light. Rube ran his fingers down the slide and over the bell, almost like he was seeing a trombone for the first time.

"So Kori," Rube finally said, "tell me, how do you take care of Russell?"

"Well," I began, "when I finish playing, I empty the spit valve. And I clean out the mouthpiece."

"With a brush?"

"Yep." I nodded. "Because there's this one kid in band who never cleans his mouthpiece. It's like some kind of science experiment. You should come to the band room some time to see the crud growing in there."

"That's quite all right." Rube held up one hand. "But thank you for the invitation."

"Sure." I smiled and went on about Russell's care. "I also grease the slide when it needs it, and I wipe off my fingerprints before I put Russell away."

"That's good," Rube said. "Real good. Now has this dent been in the bell ever since you've had it?"

"There's a dent in the bell?" I picked it up and looked all over it. "Where? I don't see it." Maybe Rube was seeing things.

"I can feel it." Rube took the bell and held it up to the light again. "But to see it, I have to hold the bell just right." He slowly turned it round and round in the light. "Aha!" Rube pointed. "You see it?"

I leaned in closer, and Rube really wasn't just seeing things. I saw it, too. "Yep, right there."

"It's just a ping dent. Don't worry. I can get that smoothed right out for you with a dent roller."

"Really? That would be so great," I said. Jack would probably never spot such a tiny dent, but I didn't want to chance it. It'd just give him more to bug me about. And he already had plenty.

"Now, when did you last give Russell a bath?" Rube went on.

"A bath?" I said.

"You know, soap, water, a bathtub. Trombones are like dogs." Rube nodded toward Mel, grinning. "They both need a good bath every now and then."

"I've never given him a bath," I admitted.

"Well, there you go, Kori. Russell is in need of a little TLC." Rube checked his watch. "If you've got some time, we'll have him fine as frog's hair."

I nodded, and Rube asked June to take over a while longer.

"June looks a lot like you, Rube," I said.

"She should!" Rube laughed. "June's my sister. She's helping me out until I can get someone in here to help manage the store."

"I saw the Help Wanted sign in the window," I said.

Rube nodded. "You wouldn't believe how hard it is to find good help these days, especially somebody I can trust. And somebody who doesn't just have a passion for music, but also knows a little something about being a manager."

"Hey, I know somebody like that," I said.

"You do?" Rube looked surprised.

"Yeah," I said. "My mom. She doesn't manage a store, but she's assistant manager at Willard's Wash and Dry Laundromat. And she works at a diner in the evenings and some weekends."

Rube nodded. "Does she love music?"

"She played clarinet in marching band in high school. And," I added, "sometimes she turns up the music on the car radio and sings so loud my little sister tells her to turn it down."

Rube reached into his back pocket and pulled out his wallet. He handed me his business card. "Would you mind giving this to your mother?"

"Sure!" I said. But I didn't even wait that long. I texted Mom to let her know I'd be later than I'd thought. And to tell her about the job opening at Rube's shop. The bells on the door jingled then. When I turned around, I saw Lem.

"Hey! Guess what?" I said.

"Hmm . . ." Lem closed his eyes. "My guess is that since you're standing in this music shop, you're not at home practicing your challenge music. Am I right, *mademoiselle*?" His eyes flew open. "*Oui*, I'm right! You're still here."

"Very funny." I frowned. "But no. Rube is helping me get a dent out of Russell and shine him up."

Rube came up behind us then, shaking his head. "No, I'm not."

"You're not?" Had Rube already changed his mind?

"I'm not shining him up." Rube pointed to me. And then pointed to himself. "*We're* shining him up. You *and* me." Rube grinned.

I smiled, too.

"Once you learn how, you can do it on your own. C'mon," Rube said, grabbing Russell. "Your friend can come, too, if he'd like."

I looked at Lem.

"Sure," he said.

So I introduced Lem to Rube. Then we followed Rube behind the counter and across the break room to an oversized sink in one corner.

Rube ran water into the sink. "Think of it like bathing a baby. You don't want the water too hot because that's not good for the finish." He held his wrist under the faucet. "Lukewarm is just right."

I let some of the water splash on my wrist, too. Then Rube handed me a towel.

"Kori, put this towel on the bottom of the sink. We don't want Russell to get any more scratches, do we?"

"No, sir!" I said, spreading the towel out flat.

When all of Russell's pieces lay on the towel, Rube shut off the water. While the slide soaked, he showed me how to clean Russell's bell and inner slide with soap and a cleaning snake with bristles.

"Now," Rube said, "rinse off the bell, and put it on that towel over there to dry, Kori."

While I rinsed the bell, Lem spread another towel on the counter beside the sink. Then Rube showed me how to clean the tuning slide and the inner slide.

"Be sure to run water through the tubes until it runs clear," Rube instructed. "And then set them on the towel to dry with the bell."

After that, we cleaned the outer slide.

"Let me show you how to use a slide cleaning rod and cheesecloth," Rube said, threading the

cloth through an eye at one end of the hook. Then he gently pulled the cloth through the tubing to clean it.

All that was left to do was clean my mouthpiece with soap, water, and a soft-bristled mouthpiece brush. Then we towel-dried the outside of all the parts and put more grease on the tuning slides and slide oil on the inner slide.

"I almost forgot, Kori," Rube said. "Let me get that dent out of your bell." So he used a dent roller and kept holding the bell up to the light to rub his fingertips across it. When Rube was finally satisfied, he said, "Smooth as can be. Now let's shine Russell right up." We used a special polish good for clear finishes.

After that, Rube gave me a few pointers about practicing lip slurs every day for even better range and breath control. And about using enough lip pressure on the mouthpiece to get a good seal, but without stifling the tone. Then I played a few measures of the song we'd worked on at practice with Mr. Byrd this afternoon.

Lem snapped his fingers, and Rube bobbed his head to the beat.

"Hoo-wee!" Rube said when I finished. "Russell may be old, but he's still got it. And so do you, Kori."

"Thanks, Rube!"

He nodded. "This old trombone has surely given the gift of music to a lot of people over the years. And if you take care of it, it still has a lot of years left. In fact, some musicians are so attached to their old instruments, you couldn't *give* 'em a new one."

"*Oui*, it kind of makes me wish my trumpet were older," Lem said. "It's sort of cool to think about who might've played your trombone before you."

"That's true." Rube smiled. "Take pride in having a vintage instrument."

"Vintage? Really?" Mom and I hunted for deals at thrift shops all the time, but Rube was right. I already had my own second-hand treasure. I don't know why I'd never thought of Russell that way before. But from now on, I would.

"Now you listen to this old man, and don't let anybody tell you any different," Rube continued, "Russell is one spiffy T-bone!"

And I had to agree. Russell was pretty spiffy. I couldn't wait to get home to practice my challenge music for our Summer Celebration concert of the school year. And I couldn't wait until band practice tomorrow. Russell would shine. And Jack would be surprised.

Chapter 8

SCHOOL LOANERS vs. THE STINKER

The next day at band practice we were assembling our instruments. Baylor was the first to notice that something was up. "Is there something, I don't know, different about you, Kori?" she asked.

Hope noticed, too. "Yeah, you do look different. Did you get a haircut?" She guessed.

I shook my head.

Baylor looked me up and down. "I got it! A new outfit?"

"Nope," I said.

"Then what?" Hope asked.

"There's nothing new about me." I smiled. And then I held up Russell.

"Kori!" Baylor squealed. "Is that a new trombone?"

"Duh! Of course it isn't," Jack jumped in before I could say anything. "Didn't you see her walk in with the same moldy old case?"

Nobody answered Jack, though. By then, other people had gathered around to see Russell. Mr. Byrd stepped off the podium for a closer look, too.

"Wow!" Mr. Byrd said. "Russell looks amazing!"

"Thank you, sir," I said.

"Did you spray-paint it?" Zac asked. "Because I have some camouflage spray paint you could've borrowed."

"No, I didn't use spray paint." But picturing Russell camouflaged made me laugh.

"Hey, that gives me an idea," Zac said. "I might just give my sax a camo makeover."

"No, you won't." Mr. Byrd shook his head. "There's no camo allowed in my band."

"Hey, I can totally picture you decked out in camo, Byrd," Zac joked. "We could call you Sergeant Byrd."

"Sergeant Byrd, huh?" He pretended to think about it. "It does have a nice ring to it, actually."

"And you do allow camo in your band," Zac said, pointing to the cap and shirt he was wearing.

"Okay, let me rephrase that. There are no camouflage *instruments* allowed in my band. So back to Russell . . . ?" Mr. Byrd continued.

"I stopped by Jazz Front," I said.

"Oh, the new music store?" Sherman asked. "I've been in there. It's funky." And he did this

weird dance move where he hopped around like a kangaroo and shook his shoulders from side to side, all at the same time. I guessed that was Sherman's attempt at being funky.

"Yeah, it's really cool," I said. "So I stopped in, and Rube Chenault helped me shine Russell up."

"Rube Chenault?" Baylor said. "I love his music. My grandpa has, like, every one of his CDs."

"Rube's awesome," I agreed. "He remembered me from the auditions to help you choose a soloist for the governor's mansion competition, Mr. Byrd."

"How kind of Rube to be willing to help you out, Kori! And seriously, Russell has never looked better," Mr. Byrd said.

Then he headed back to the podium. "Okay, folks. Time's wasting here. Let's bop the concert B-flat scale."

Everyone scrambled back to their seats and warm-ups began. We played a few scales and tuned our instruments. Then Mr. Byrd hopped off the podium again, this time to work one-on-one with the percussion section in the back of the room.

Jack glanced around to make sure Mr. Byrd was out of earshot before opening his mouth. "I don't see what the big deal is about Rube Chenault. That old guy is clueless. I can't believe he'd help you." Jack shook his head. "What's the big deal, anyway? You polished your old trombone. So what?"

When I didn't say anything, Jack laughed. Not a laugh because anything was funny, either. A mean laugh.

Jack was wrong about Rube. He wasn't clueless. At all. He was awesome.

But Jack was right about Russell. Russell was shinier now, but he was still the same old school loaner I played yesterday. And last month. And even last year. I wasn't sure why Rube and I even shined up Russell in the first place. Seriously, why bother?

But then I thought about what Rube had said about Russell being vintage. And a spiffy T-bone. And how so many musicians had played Russell before me. He said not to let anybody tell me any different. Maybe Rube meant Jack.

But Jack wasn't finished yet. "It's still just school-loaner junk. And you can't change that."

I looked at Jack then.

His eyes narrowed. "Can you?"

"No, Jack. I can't," I said.

He sat back and grinned, like he'd just won.

But this time, I wasn't done either. "You know what? I don't want to change it. Russell is special. He has history. And character. And Mrs. Friddell says the way people act says a lot about their character."

"Wait," Jack said. "Who's Mrs. Friddell? And what's that even supposed to mean?"

"Mrs. Friddell lives in the apartment next door. She helps out when my mom has to work. And she calls people who aren't being so nice to other people stinkers," I explained. "And you're never nice to me in band. So you, Jack Cassilly III, are a stinker."

"Tell him!" Zac turned around and clapped then. "Quiet Kori isn't so quiet anymore! Keep going!"

Lem shot me a thumbs-up, and Hope and Baylor both smiled.

But Jack frowned. I knew he probably wasn't finished bugging me about Russell. But that was okay. Because Baylor was right. I had sort of found my voice. I really wasn't Quiet Kori anymore. And because for now, in the game of the School Loaners vs. the Stinker, the score was 1–0.

That's kind of how I felt, too. Like I'd just scored a game-winning shot right before the buzzer rang out across the gym. And like I hadn't just stood up for me and Russell, but for band kids all over the world. Okay, maybe that was a stretch. But really,

I did feel like I'd stood up for everyone else in the band who had a school loaner, too.

The other school-loaner kids! I suddenly felt really bad for them. We started the fund-raisers to help us all get new instruments. But Pampered Pets and the garage sale hadn't been hits. So now other kids, like Kelly and Alex, wouldn't be getting new instruments like they'd hoped. Unless . . .

I had the perfect idea! And as soon as the bell rang, I talked to Mr. Byrd about it.

Chapter 9

CHENAULT'S CARE CLINIC

"So how are you doing with your challenge music?" Lem asked the next week when we stood outside the band room before practice. "We don't have much time until the concert, you know."

"Two weeks," I said. "I circled it on the calendar. And the challenge music is going great."

"Really?" Lem asked.

"Yep. Mrs. Friddell has been helping out while Mom's working. So I've been practicing a lot." I smiled. "But in a few days, I can practice even more. Like I used to."

"How come, *mademoiselle*?" Lem asked.

"Did you notice the Help Wanted sign was taken out of the window at Rube's shop?"

He shook his head.

"Yep, it's gone. That's because he hired my mom to work there as the manager. And she'll make more money, so she can quit working two jobs now."

"Kori!" Lem held up his hand for a high-five. "That's awesome! This'll be the best Summer Celebration concert ever!"

"Definitely!" I agreed.

"With you in it, more like the worst," Jack said, shuffling past us.

I frowned.

"Forget Jack," Lem said. "He's just jealous, especially since he found out Rube was helping you after he already turned Jack down."

"Wait," I said. "Rube turned Jack down for what?"

But Mr. Byrd was already starting practice, so Lem and I hurried inside the band room. I'd have to remember to ask Lem later what he meant.

Practice started out pretty ordinary. Yulia was new to band this year, and she always had some problem with her clarinet. Pretty much every day. Still. Today she asked, "Is my reed supposed to look like that?"

"Uh, no," Baylor told her. "It's chipped."

So we stopped for Yulia to change out reeds. Then she complained that her clarinet wouldn't play F. But when she blew into it and held down the correct keys, it did. "Well, normally it doesn't," she said.

And then Davis and a couple of other students had lost their sheet music, so Mr. Byrd had to make some extra copies. Another typical day in the band room.

Finally, everyone was ready. We practiced a couple of our songs for the concert. And Mr. Byrd seemed happy with the way we played. "Good things are happening here, folks!" he said. "Now you're playing like the musicians you are!"

About halfway through practice, though, someone knocked on the band room door.

"Excuse me," Mr. Byrd said, stepping into the hallway. When he came back in, he wasn't alone. Rube was with him.

"Hey, it's Rube Chenault!" "Rube Chenault's here!" Excited voices bounced off the band room's concrete walls.

"Settle down, everyone," Mr. Byrd said. "I see you all remember Mr. Chenault, our favorite jazz musician. But in case you didn't know, he's also now the owner of the newly opened Jazz Front music shop. Let's show Mr. Chenault we're glad he's here today."

Everybody clapped. And I even whistled.

"Well, now," Rube said when the applause died down. "That's a warm welcome if I ever saw one. Thank you, boys and girls." Then he turned to Mr. Byrd and shook his hand. "And thank you for inviting me into your wonderful band room."

"The pleasure is ours, sir," Mr. Byrd said. "Thank you for being so gracious with your time to pay us a visit."

"Yes, indeed," Rube said.

"So Mr. Chenault, should we tell them why you're here today?"

"I don't know." Rube looked out into the band room. "What do you all think?"

More shouts of "Yeah!" and "Tell us!" erupted.

Lem leaned forward in his chair and waved at me to catch my attention. When I looked at him, he raised one eyebrow. I smiled. Yep, I already knew why Rube was here. And Lem must've figured out I had something to do with it.

"Okay, okay." Mr. Byrd held up both hands. "Kori Neal recently got some excellent pointers for instrument care from Mr. Chenault. So she suggested that it might be beneficial for the rest of you to get some tips, too."

"That's right," Rube said. "Where is Kori?"

I waved my hand as he scanned the room.

"Ah, there she is," Rube said, waving back.

"So anyway," Mr. Byrd continued, "that's how the idea for an instrument care clinic was born. Mr. Chenault, please take it away."

"Thank you. But first, please call me Rube. Mr. Chenault makes me sound like an old man." He patted his gray hair. "Never mind, I am an old man. But call me Rube anyway, please."

I wasn't the only one who laughed then.

"Today," Rube went on, "I'd like to begin with a simple question. Why should you take care of your instrument?"

Hands started flying up to answer the question.

"Yes, young lady?" Rube pointed at Hope.

"Because we signed up for band, so we're responsible for taking care of our instruments," Hope said.

"Responsible. I like that word." Rube nodded. "Being in band does teach responsibility, doesn't it? It's not an individual sport, but a group effort. Your band director and the entire band counts on you." He pointed at us. "So be responsible for taking care of your instrument to keep it in good working order. And be responsible enough to bring it to practice. Don't leave it on the bus."

"Zac!" I heard Baylor whisper. He is always forgetting his saxophone, at least, he always uses "I forgot it" for his excuse.

"Are there any other reasons you should care for your instrument?" Rube went on.

"Because if we don't, our parents will kill us," Zac blurted out.

Rube grinned. "I don't think they'd kill you, son, but they would be pretty mad, now wouldn't they?"

"Yeah, because they're expensive," Jack chimed in. Then he said for my ears only, "At least, good instruments are."

Rube nodded again. "Some instruments are expensive, young man. They cost a small fortune.

Others aren't as expensive. But they're still wonderful instruments."

Jack's whispering was no match for Rube's hearing. Rube glanced around. "Anyone else?"

Nobody said anything.

Rube cleared his throat. "I want every one of you to hold up your instruments. Go on now. Hold them up there." He looked back at the percussion section. "You drummers, in the back, don't try to be cute. You just hold up your sticks."

All around the room, clarinets and flutes and trumpets and other instruments were going up.

"Now take a look at yourselves," Rube said. "What do you have in your hands, boys and girls? Think about it, and I'll ask you again at the end of the workshop."

"Now," he said, walking over to the white board, "put your instruments down, and we'll review some basic instrument care. What's number one?"

"Don't drop your instrument," Sherman said.

"That could be bad," Rube agreed. "Have any of you ever seen a flute that's been left on the floor and then accidentally stepped on?" He shivered. "It's not a pretty sight. So remember, if your instrument's not on your face, keep it in your case."

Rube scrawled Case with a red marker. "Drummers, this doesn't apply to you."

Next, Rube wrote Sugar. "You might be scratching your head, wondering what on Earth and Jupiter I'm talking about.

"But the sugars in the foods you eat and the things you drink not only can harm you, they can harm your instrument, corroding the inside of it, damaging reeds and mouthpieces, and even wearing out parts, like pads, quicker."

Then he circled Sugar on the board and drew a line through it. "No sugar while you're playing. If you're thirsty, grab some water. It's better for you. And for your instrument."

"And no gum while you play either," Zac added.

"Oh, yes," Mr. Byrd said. "Zac found that out the hard way. Didn't you, Zac?"

Zac grinned and nodded.

"Yes, siree," Rube said. "It's true. Gum is no friend to instruments." Then he wrote Gum beside Sugar. "Any guesses for number three?"

Nobody said anything.

Rube drew an arrow back up to case. "This goes back to number one. The case is not your storage place. You brass players are going for a world record. How many tubes of valve oil can be stuffed into one case? And with others, it's your reeds." He pretended to turn a steering wheel. "The folks from Guinness pull up, and you tell them you have 829 reeds in your case!"

"That's Yulia," Baylor said. "She practically has a reed collection in her case, all chipped!"

When people stopped laughing at that one, Rube said, "And some of you turn your case into a mobile locker. You stuff calculators and rulers and pencils in there. So if a break-out math session pops up between measures, you'll be prepared."

I pointed at Lem and he rolled his eyes. He was a math whiz. And we all knew if we needed to borrow a pencil, Lem kept extras in his case.

"And don't forget sheet music," Rube went on. "You're like, 'How many pieces of sheet music can

I fit in this case before the hinges pop off?'" He grinned. "You're just waiting for one to go flying through the air. And score extra points if it lands on your band director's desk."

Kids started laughing again.

"Now you can laugh, but you know what I'm talking about. Seriously, now," Rube continued, "storing personal items in your case can bend your keys. So please, don't use your case for storage."

He turned around and wrote Repairs. "This is important. Don't try to repair a broken instrument yourself. And this applies to you, too, drummers." He pointed toward the back. "There are people out there who have studied for years to learn how to correctly repair instruments. Please, please, please take your instrument to someone with experience when it comes to repairs. Okay?

"Your instrument will thank you for years to come. And that's how long they should last—for years and years." Rube capped the marker he was holding and set it aside. "Any questions?"

Nobody raised a hand.

"You all are just soaking everything in, aren't you?" Rube smiled. "That's good. Now we're going to discuss some tips that are unique to different instruments. We'll start with woodwinds."

Rube talked about never picking up instruments by their keys and never forcing the parts together. Then he moved on to the brass section and discussed the importance of opening the spit valves and blowing through the instruments to remove excess moisture every day and keeping the slides and valves lubricated on a regular basis.

After that, Rube told the drummers to be sure their drums were secure on their stands and not to set objects on their drums. "Don't use your instrument for a table," he said.

Then Rube talked more about the importance of cleaning and gave us some tips, before checking out everyone's instruments. He even helped us tune them.

When he was finished, Mr. Byrd asked, "Would you like a preview of our Summer Celebration concert?"

"I'd love one!" Rube grinned.

So we ran through our songs for Rube, and he clapped when we were done. "Hoo-wee! Excellent job, boys and girls!"

"Thanks for all of your help, Rube," Mr. Byrd said. "The band has never sounded better."

"I'm excited about the music being made in this room," Rube said. "And before I take off, remember I asked you earlier to hold up your instruments? Well, by now, I hope you understand you hold so much more than an instrument in your hands."

Rube paused to look around the room before continuing. "It's the gift of music. It's powerful. When you play your instrument, you have the power. You can move people. Take care of your gift!"

Mr. Byrd clapped then. And the rest of us clapped, too.

"That old guy is crazy," Jack whispered. "No wonder he hung out with you and your dumb trombone, Kori."

It was easy to ignore Jack, though, because Rube wasn't finished talking yet. "Now, just one last thing. I have a surprise for you, boys and girls," he said, smiling.

Chapter 10
RUBE'S SURPRISE

"Kori told me about the band's recent fund-raisers to raise money for some new instruments," Rube began. "Even though you didn't raise as much as you'd hoped, I admire your gumption. That's the kind of people I like working with. In fact, for those of you with school-loaner instruments, I'd like the honor of working with you myself."

Alex looked at me from the French horn section. I shrugged. I had no idea what Rube meant.

"So I'd like to offer you lessons during summer break." Rube looked at Mr. Byrd. "Could I borrow a sheet of paper, sir?"

"Absolutely!" Mr. Byrd handed Rube a piece of paper and a pen.

"Thank you," Rube said, holding up the paper. "This will be our sign-up sheet for the lessons. All you have to do is sign your name here, and I'll get back with you as far as dates and times. Sound good?"

It did sound good. But there was one small problem.

I raised my hand.

"Kori?" Rube said.

"How much are lessons?" I wasn't sure about everyone else, but I definitely couldn't afford private lessons.

"Oh, did I leave out that small detail?" Rube grinned. "They're free!"

Alex looked at me again and mouthed, "*Free?*"

I nodded.

Alex jumped out of his chair. "Sign me up!" he said, rushing to the front of the band room.

"Hey, Alex! Sign me up, too, please!" Then I mumbled to myself, "I can't believe this."

But Jack heard me. "Me either." He sounded upset. "That's not fair. I wish I had private lessons."

"You already do. Remember?" I said.

"I do." Jack frowned. "But not with Rube Chenault."

"So what? You just called Rube crazy five minutes ago. Did you forget that, too?"

Jack didn't say anything.

"Are you okay?" I wasn't really sure why I cared. And I really, really wasn't sure why I suddenly felt sorry for Jack, of all people. He'd been a real jerk to me. But today, there was a sad look in his big blue eyes that I'd never seen there before. "Jack? Are you okay?" I asked again, softer this time.

He shook his head. "Not really."

"Wanna talk about it?" I held my breath in case this was when Jack decided to explode.

Jack looked at me then. I wasn't completely sure, but I thought his eyes looked sort of wet. "No." He blinked. Then, "Yeah. Maybe."

"Is this like multiple choice? No, yeah, or maybe? Should I circle one?" I smiled a little. "Cause I circle B for yeah. What's going on?"

"I've been a real jerk lately, Kori."

I wanted to say something sarcastic, like "Really? I hadn't noticed!" Or maybe even clap and give Jack a standing ovation. But I decided to keep my mouth shut and listen.

"I know maybe I've even been sort of mean sometimes."

I nodded.

"And I'm sorry."

Okay, I really didn't see that coming.

"I guess I was sort of jealous," Jack went on.

What? Jack Cassilly III was jealous of *me*? He was the one with the best of everything—clothes, instrument, private lessons, and a Mom and Dad that were loaded.

And most importantly his mom and dad were still married. To each other.

"Why would you ever be jealous of me?" I asked.

"Because. You know how you told me once that money couldn't buy talent?"

"Yeah," I said. "But I didn't mean that you don't have talent, Jack. Because you do." And I wasn't just saying that either. It was true. Jack was great at trombone.

He shook his head. "Maybe. But not as good as you, Kori. I tried to get a new instrument and private lessons to be better than you. I even tried to get lessons with Rube. But he was busy opening his new store."

So that's what Lem meant when he said before class that Rube had turned Jack down.

"But," Jack went on, "when I heard you and Lem practice your challenge music a few minutes ago, I knew you were a natural. No money needed."

"But being a natural only goes so far, you know. It takes a lot of practice, too. And I know you practice a lot. You really are great on trombone, Jack." But I got the feeling there was something more. "This isn't all about new trombones and private lessons." I almost whispered, "Is it?"

"Nope." Jack swallowed hard. "Money can't keep my parents together either."

"What do you mean?"

"I may as well get used to telling people, I guess. So you're the first to know." He took a deep breath. "My parents split up a few weeks ago. And today, they filed for divorce."

It was a few weeks ago when Jack suddenly turned into Band Jerk Jack. And now I knew why. When my dad left, I hadn't been so nice either. Not to anybody, not my brother, my sisters, or my mom, even.

"I'm sorry, Jack. If it helps, I get how you feel right now. And it'll get better. Trust me."

"I know. And thanks."

"For what?" I asked.

"For still talking to me after the way I acted."

I shrugged. "No big deal," I said. "Just don't act like a jerk again. Got it?"

Jack tried to smile.

"I have one more announcement," Rube said then. "Nine people have signed up for lessons. Let's make it an even ten. Kori, could you choose someone?"

Hands went up all around the band.

"Maybe you should select a trombonist," Rube added. "Then you two could work together, too."

A few hands dropped then, since they didn't play trombone. That really narrowed it down and made my choice easier.

"I pick Jack," I said.

"Seriously?" Jack asked.

"Yeah," I said.

I wasn't sure who was more surprised, Jack or me. "Unless you're too busy with your other lessons."

"No, I can cancel those. Honestly, they were with a high-school kid who didn't even play that great."

"And," I added, "if you don't mind hanging out with me and Russell."

Jack laughed. It was a real laugh, too, not a mean laugh, like before. He even had a cute dimple in one cheek that I'd never noticed before.

When I first stopped by Rube's shop, I thought it was kind of like an ending to a story because I couldn't get a new trombone. You know, The End. But it wasn't. Really, it was just the beginning. Sort of like opening the page to Chapter One.

And as the story went along, Quiet Kori sort of disappeared. And I became better friends with Lem, Baylor, Hope, and Zac. I even made a new, old friend—Rube.

Now there was Jack, too. We weren't exactly friends yet. But the way he was smiling at me, we definitely could be.

I'd also realized how important my old friend Russell was to me. Way too important to ever get rid of. What was I thinking? My trombone might be second hand, but it was still first class.